Large Animal Games

by Steve Yockey

A SAMUEL FRENCH ACTING EDITION

SAMUEL FRENCH

FOUNDED 1830

NEW YORK HOLLYWOOD LONDON TORONTO

SAMUELFRENCH.COM

ISBN 978-0-573-69849-1   Printed in U.S.A.   #29662

MUSIC USE NOTE

**IMPORTANT BILLING AND CREDIT
REQUIREMENTS**

LARGE ANIMAL GAMES opened on Nov 6, 2009 as a co-world premiere at the Dad's Garage Top Shelf Theatre in Atlanta, Georgia. Produced by Dad's Garage Theatre Company (Scott Warren, Artistic Producer; Lena Carstens, Managing Director). Directed by Melissa Foulger. The cast was as follows:

JIMMY	Joe Sykes
ALICIA	Whittney Millsap
STAN	Clint Sowell
ROSE	Erin Burnett
NICOLE	Alison Hastings
MIGUEL	Louis Gregory
VALERIE	Shannon Byrd
Scenic Design	Oz Dillman
Lighting	Ben Tilley
Sound	Rene Delefont
Costumes	Liz Faughnan

LARGE ANIMAL GAMES opened on Nov 7, 2009 as a co-world premiere at LaVal's Subterranean Theatre in Berkeley, California. Produced by Impact Theatre with (Melissa Hillman, Artistic Director; Cheshire Isaacs, Managing Director). Directed by Melissa Hillman. The cast was as follows:

JIMMY	Jai Sahai
ALICIA	Marissa Keltie
STAN	Timothy Redmond
ROSE	Elisa Dunn
NICOLE	Cindy Im
MIGUEL	Roy Landaverde
VALERIE	Leontyne Mbele-Mbong
Scenic Design	Sarah Coykendall
Lighting	Jacqueline Steager
Sound	Colin Trevor
Costumes	Virginia Thorne

CHARACTERS

ROSE – A woman, twenties; lots of hope, lots of plans, lots to say about everything. A total fan of anything she can pair with a smart skirt. Not a good listener.

NICOLE – A woman, twenties; far too analytical for her surroundings. Hipster stylish, but not as cool as she thinks. Poor timing. And probably not a good judge of men.

MIGUEL – A man from Spain, early twenties; sexy, along for the ride. Sweetly, innocently unkempt, jeans, shirt, but everything is appropriately tight, he is basically a fantasy.

ALICIA – A woman, late twenties; attractive, self-assured, appearance, appearance & more appearance. Not in a bad way, just a fact. Every little detail is in place. Every one.

STAN – A man, late twenties; attractive, an everyman, almost perfect. Almost. Button up shirt and slacks. Probably glasses, but they look good. Confident.

VALERIE – An African-American woman, thirties; "othered" in her own life, no nonsense and looking for answers abroad. Dressed for travel, maybe a hat.

JIMMY – A man, ageless but still young; dry, unexpected, wise but casual. White V-neck T-shirt, jeans, maybe some colored tennis shoes, a measuring tape around his neck and a pencil behind his ear. Magical, but nothing overt.

AUTHOR'S NOTES

[ ] indicate overlapping dialogue.

The style and tone of the piece are definitely "heightened."

Except for the props and pieces that the cast members manipulate, the stage is relatively bare. Lights and sound go a long way towards shaping the space. Scenes should flow together quickly, seamlessly.

"Beauty depends on size as well as symmetry. No very small animal can be beautiful; for looking at it takes so small a portion of time that the impression of it will be confused. Nor can any very large one, for a whole view of it cannot be had at once."

– Aristotle

1

(JIMMY *enters the bare stage in dim light. He pulls a single rack of colorful lingerie behind him. Once he gets it set in just the right place, he turns and takes in the audience.*)

JIMMY. I'm sure I've got something that will fit you just right. Make you feel beautiful. Special. Make someone else get a little "hot and bothered" or whatever colorful colloquial euphemism you prefer. So what do you think? Quite a collection, every single one hand made. I know because I make them. Okay, and also these two near-sighted elderly women that sew really well, but mostly I make them, for our purposes, just think of me as the guy who makes them.

We specialize in the custom fit, just like a second skin, something to make you feel special. Measurements, measurements, every single piece stitched precisely to your need. Because sometimes the small things become big things and the big things become small things and everything in between, you know?

Of course, it only works when you know what you need. You'd be amazed at how many people come in here with no idea what they're looking for at all. Amazed. No idea. None.

(JIMMY *takes in the audience and then gestures into the air. Suddenly music fills the space, something poppy and danceable and entirely fun like Kylie Minogue's "WOW"* as the lights shift and wash over the stage. Maybe there's even a disco ball. It is loud and fun.*)

(*All of the characters begin entering in a line from one*

* Please See Music Use Note on Page 3.

side of the space carrying a chair, prop, or item of cloth-
ing that will be used in the play. They cross the stage
delivering the item to its location and continuing off
the opposite side. But it's more energetic than it sounds,
frenetic even. They're enjoying this. Like a never-ending
parade, equally spaced, no gaps, building the playing
areas. Spare, easy, but clear.)

(The first two areas are apartments, one belonging to
Rose and the other to Stan. Rose's apartment is a few
chairs and a large amount of luggage. Stan's apartment
is a small couch and a table.)

(The third area is a lingerie shop indicated by a stool
next to a counter with the single rack of colorful lingerie
behind it.)

(Near the counter is some type of pole, about 7 feet high
or so, with a little extension arm on it. Like an upside
down 'L.' At the end of the arm hangs a small bell, like
the kind that might hang on a store door to let the shop-
keeper know someone had entered. Jimmy exists in the
space for most of the play, observing the action in the
different areas as it unfolds. Use discretion in deciding
when he should be absent.)

(The final area built is a row of chairs just on stage,
equal to the number of actors, a staging area of sorts
with most of the things that will be needed for the play.
If playing space is an issue, the actors can simply enter
and exit form off stage.)

(As the set takes shape, the music fades as the characters
each into their chair, except Alicia. **JIMMY** *hangs on the*
edge of the stage and motions towards the opposite side.)

(ALICIA *enters carrying a shopping bag from some*
department store. She sets the bag down next to her feet,
removes her sunglasses and lets her purse fall from her
shoulder into her hand, hooking the sunglasses over
the strap. It's a practiced thing, no thought. **JIMMY**
vanishes.)

(ALICIA smiles. She is poised and it is effortless, casual and warm.)

ALICIA. Shopping can take a lot out of you, right? Not like it's saving the world or anything, I'm not making any lofty comparisons; I'm not contrasting a credit card swipe to joining Médecins Sans Frontières or anything. Just, it can be actually exhausting trying to find just the right thing. Especially when it's important. Like… when you're getting married, for instance. And I am. So it's not even a hypothetical, which is so crazy.

(She laughs and shows off her engagement ring as JIMMY approaches with two additional shopping bags. He drops the bags off next to her single bag, takes a brief look at the ring and offers this quick exchange while moving through and disappearing again.)

JIMMY. Nice.

ALICIA. Isn't it?

JIMMY. Perfect.

(And he's gone.)

ALICIA. Stan, my fiancé, picked out a ring that was so beautiful; he has excellent taste. But of course he knew better than to buy it on his own. We went and looked at it and then we decided this one was just a bit more, well, I don't want to say 'appropriate' because that sounds so officious, but this one is more, something like, indicative of our love. And the diamond is bigger. Because you don't want a ring you have to explain. You want a ring that answers all those questions on its own. You want a ring that doesn't evoke questioning at all. Some people would say it's superficial.

JIMMY. *(dropping off two more shopping bags next to her…)* Mm hm.

ALICIA. It's not. It's not, but it sounds so abstract, right? Or at least not very important, but it's not unimportant, it's very important. It just sounds very, oh, no, like this, this is more concrete: I sit down to lunch with a friend, whoever, it doesn't matter. And she notices my Hermès bag. And why wouldn't she, it's gorgeous.

JIMMY. *(dropping off two more bags next to her...)* Gorgeous.

ALICIA. Yes. But I can tell she's thinking, "That can't be a real Hermès bag." And I just want to say, "Shut your fucking mouth!" But of course I can't because she didn't actually say anything. But she knows I know what she thinks. We know. That's what I'm talking about. And it would be so much easier and a lot less energy expended if I didn't care and isn't that just what everyone says and blah, blah, blah.

*(**JIMMY** laughs along with her, or maybe at her a bit, while dropping off two more bags...)*

JIMMY. See you later.

ALICIA. Oh, um, okay.

*(As **JIMMY** exits, she whispers conspiratorially:)*

It is so awkward when retail people make chitchat isn't it? Well not, you know what I mean.

(back at full voice)

Anyway, about my bag, now it would be another thing all together if she thought it was a fake bag and it was a fake bag and I knew it, she knew it and oh my god, I can't even imagine how embarrassing. But it's not a fake bag so I'm right, she's wrong and she can go choke on all of her unspoken aspersions.

(No, she's calm; it's okay.)

And then we have a nice lunch. Because I'm better at that game, my choices are unassailable. Whatever she might whisper about me, it's not true.

(She puts on her sunglasses, shoulders her purse and collects all of the shopping bags.)

So that's how I win.

(She exits.)

End Scene

2

(NICOLE stands in Rose's apartment as ROSE pours two Jameson's on ice. There are two chairs, a small table and a large pile of luggage. It's really more like an impossibly huge pile of luggage.)

ROSE. It was thrilling. And he had this red, I don't know, cape, but not around his neck. It was over his arm and he used it to steer the bull around, or really just to make the bull angry. Kind of taunting it?

NICOLE. Where is that sound coming from?

ROSE. I'm trying to tell you about this bullfight.

NICOLE. Is someone in your shower?

ROSE. What? No, it's the pipes. We have noisy pipes.

NICOLE. Noisy pipes?

ROSE. Valerie complains about it all the time, but to be fair, she complains about everything.

NICOLE. And where is she again?

ROSE. Who cares, not here. I will never get a roommate from the paper again. Go away newspaper ad roommate, go away.

NICOLE. You have to get them from [somewhere.]

ROSE. [Well, when] she gets back, I'm having a talk with her about maybe finding a new place. About her finding a new place.

NICOLE. Oh.

ROSE. Now, can I finish my story?

NICOLE. I don't understand, where did she go?

ROSE. Ugh.

(She drinks the glass of Jameson's down.)

She went to Africa. Don't ask me. I tried to talk to her about it but she's so angry all the time. I think it's like a quest to find her roots or something; to find her "home," I don't know.

NICOLE. She said that?

ROSE. Not exactly. She said she needed to get away.

NICOLE. And, let me follow you on this, because she's black you infer that she's going to Africa to experience a transformative homecoming? Is that right?

ROSE. What?

NICOLE. Casual racism.

ROSE. Shut-up.

NICOLE. I'm just saying that [it's not...]

ROSE. [No, I'm] just saying, who "gets away" to Africa? You know what I mean. Ah ah, you know what I mean. She's been so depressed and moody, breakfast around here is like a funeral march. So a vacation, whatever kind of vacation, will do her good. Mine sure did.

NICOLE. You do look sunny.

*(**ROSE** pours another glass with a big smile.)*

ROSE. I do, I know. So okay, there's dust everywhere, dirt from the arena or whatever, and this guy was just stunningly graceful as he led the bull around the ring, charge after charge. I felt myself get, well, I was afraid for him, but it all seemed so effortless [really.]

NICOLE. [Most] difficult things do when an expert's [doing them.]

ROSE. [Stop] interrupting. And then at the end of it all, he kind of did this one last flourish of red through the air as the bull passed, and he took this long blade and just...

(She mimes skewering something.)

NICOLE. That sounds horrifying.

ROSE. Horrifying?

NICOLE. He, like, killed the bull?

ROSE. It wasn't horrifying, or I don't know, it was something like that but also this other thing. Almost heroic.

NICOLE. Huh.

ROSE. And Miguel, the guy, the man who took me to the fight...

NICOLE. The guy you mooned about in that postcard.

ROSE. Yes. Miguel. He held my hand during that part. I was breathing heavy in that moment before it happened and he took my hand and whispered something.

NICOLE. What did he whisper?

ROSE. I couldn't really hear him, everyone was shouting, it doesn't matter. Just feeling his breath on my ear made my heart go so fast and then the bullfighter killed the bull and there was this jolt through me and, and…and it was over. You'll never believe, I did the most impetuous thing. I still can't believe it myself, it's so out of character, really, [and I…]

NICOLE. [You slept] with him!

ROSE. No! No, don't be so crass Nicole. I wouldn't just sleep with him; I mean I wanted to, oh my god I wanted to, but not like that. This was something really special.

NICOLE. And sex isn't special?

ROSE. Ugh, that's not what I meant. Obviously sex is, see, this is what you do, you over-analyze every little thing. You can't ever just let something wash over you.

NICOLE. Oh now what's that [supposed to mean?]

ROSE. [I'm sitting here] telling you this story, this romantic, this kind of epic love story.

NICOLE. Epic?

ROSE. And you pick apart every little detail. You don't know how to just enjoy things [Nicole.]

NICOLE. [Okay, that's] sort of an exaggeration and not exactly fair.

ROSE. Ha!

NICOLE. That's not what I do. Or maybe it is, but your story has a lot of hazy "romantic" detail in it that, you know, kind of screams for clarification.

ROSE. Fine. I'm not talking to you anymore about this. Clearly you can't understand what I'm trying to explain.

NICOLE. That's not true.

(pause)

Rose, don't be mad at me. Come on, I want to hear the story. What did you do? After the bullfight what did you do?

ROSE. It's not a joke.

NICOLE. No, I know. I'll be good.

ROSE. All right. So at the end of the trip, I was getting ready to leave and I think he, I mean he had mentioned how much he'd love to visit New York City, how he'd heard about it, so I invited him to [come and...]

NICOLE. [You did] not.

ROSE. I did. I invited him to come stay here, with me, whenever he wants to, so I can show him around.

NICOLE. Uh huh.

ROSE. He's so amazing. I think he couldn't really afford to make the trip, so I told him if he ever wanted to come I would buy him a plane ticket [because I...]

NICOLE. [Okay, see,] this, this moment, this is where, as your friend, I really have to say something.

ROSE. I really wish you wouldn't.

NICOLE. You offered to buy a plane ticket for some guy you knew for, what? Two minutes? Some guy from Spain, some Spaniard?

ROSE. Now who's discriminating?

NICOLE. Oh, I don't care if he's the prince of Sweden, that's not the, ugh, my point is you don't just go offering to fly strange men, even strange, romantic, attractive bullfighters around the world because of a schoolgirl crush.

ROSE. He's not a bullfighter. And it's not a crush. You don't know, I told you that you wouldn't understand, you can't understand. It was love at first sight. Some people are capable of that. And some people...aren't.

NICOLE. Oh, stop it. Listen, I just came to welcome you home. I just came to drink some Jameson's and hear fun stories about Spain while I help you unpack. I didn't…

(She notices the suitcases.)

Are there, like, a lot of extra suitcases. This is way more [than you…]

ROSE. [No, I don't know,] what do you mean, no, don't be silly.

(pause)

NICOLE. Who's in the shower? That was the shower and Valerie's gone, noisy pipes, who's in the shower?

ROSE. Now be nice.

NICOLE. He's here, the bullfighter's here [now?]

ROSE. [He's not] a bullfighter; he took me to a bullfight.

NICOLE. I can't believe you.

ROSE. You better be nice.

NICOLE. What am I supposed to…?

*(**NICOLE** is interrupted as **MIGUEL** enters in a red towel. He stops.)*

MIGUEL. Perdòname.

ROSE. Nicole, this is Miguel. Miguel, this is my best friend Nicole.

*(**NICOLE** waves self-consciously. **MIGUEL** waves back.)*

MIGUEL. Necesito recoger algunas cosas.

*(He grabs a small bag and begins to leave; turns to **NICOLE**.)*

Eh…Me entiendes o eres como ella?

(Pause. The women simply look at him. He smiles.)

Eres tan bella. Tus ojos brillantes, tus labios, tu tez suave.

*(He crosses to **NICOLE**, takes her hand and kisses it.)*

ROSE. Well, that's "friendly."

NICOLE. I don't, [uh…]

MIGUEL. [Sí,] amor. Lo creo.

(*He disappears again.* **NICOLE** *doesn't move.*)

ROSE. Isn't he gorgeous?

NICOLE. What'd he say?

ROSE. I have no idea. I only learned about four things out of that phrase book.

NICOLE. Doesn't he speak English?

ROSE. Nope.

(**NICOLE** *snaps out of it.*)

NICOLE. He doesn't speak English?!

ROSE. Isn't it amazing? It's almost like magic that we've found each other, the two of us in this big, crowded world. We just have this, I don't know, this connection.

NICOLE. Rose, this doesn't seem like a very [good idea.]

ROSE. [We have a magical] connection and I don't want to hear another goddamn word about it.

NICOLE. But [you…]

ROSE. [Not] another word.

(*Standoff.* **NICOLE** *shrugs, conceding.*)

Good. Now, let's have another drink. He takes forever to get ready.

End Scene

3

(VALERIE stands alone.)

VALERIE. Listen, I'm not going to Africa on a spiritual journey. I'm not going to Africa to find my history. Nice to meet you. I traced my family tree once, all the way back to a bill of sale at an auction in Charleston. And before that? Nothing. How could there be really? Africa's a big place with a lot of people. A friend of mine took 15 years to track down some of his remote relatives in Nigeria, and he's still not sure that it's a legit connection. He just wants it to be. You know, one of those things. Besides, I grew up in Costa Mesa. That's who I am. So it's not like I'm going to show up in Kenya and fall to my knees crying. That's not my "home" and when people assume things about me because of, well, because of any kind of "external qualities," then that's all about them. I'm gonna' show up in Kenya the way mid-western people on vacation show up at Disneyland: ready to enjoy myself.

And the best part, oh, the best part: I'm going there to kill something. Believe it. I'm going on safari. Not just safari, a safari where they guarantee the opportunity to shoot some big game, large animals. I've been planning it for a few months and now that it's almost here, well, I can't believe it's almost here. It's been a lot of work too, all of these details, all of the negotiating: time off, airline tickets, the actual safari, my travel visa, the shots, you wouldn't believe the number of shots you have to get. But you wanna' know the hardest part? Choosing the gun.

That's a big deal. A gun to shoot at something large I mean, not like a handgun, a pistol, some little thing. I'm talking about a big gun. There's a lot of time and energy that goes into that kind of decision. I did my homework and ultimately landed on a Bolt Action Weatherby Mark V Safari Custom; French walnut and ebony with a satin oil finish. I was going to go with an adjustable trigger, really personalize it, but the standard has a pull weight of about three pounds, which feels good. And doesn't mess with my aim. That's important. I mean, it can be the prettiest gun I've ever seen, but if I can't aim it then what's the point?

I'm...I'm embarrassed to admit this, but I spent a huge chunk of my savings on it. Between the gun and the trip, about $7,000. And let's be frank, that's no small amount for me. That's not a small amount of money for anyone nowadays. But my attitude is this: if you're going to take the time to really kill something, you want to do it right.

End Scene

4

(STAN is reading the newspaper, shoes off, on the couch in his apartment. ALICIA enters with even more shopping bags, full to bursting; a lot more bags. It is clear that a ridiculous amount of shopping has occurred.)

ALICIA. I'm back.

STAN. How did it–oh my god what did you do?

ALICIA. Nothing. Shopping. Nothing.

(She tries to hide the bags behind her. He puts down the paper.)

STAN. I've already seen the bags, Alicia.

ALICIA. Okay, but these were all things we really needed. Really. No, really.

STAN. This is what happens when you go shopping with your Mom.

ALICIA. Okay, well the next round of wedding shopping, you're up to bat.

STAN. "Wedding shopping." What does that even mean?

ALICIA. It means shopping for the wedding.

STAN. But specifically, what does [it mean?]

ALICIA. [Specifically] come with me and find out.

(She leans in. He kisses her.)

STAN. No thank you.

ALICIA. Boooo to that. You're no fun.

STAN. How much of that did I pay for?

ALICIA. Okay, you're a little fun. A very little.

STAN. Thanks.

ALICIA. It's not as much as it looks like. You wanna' see?

STAN. Rose called for you; she's back from her trip to Spain.

ALICIA. Okay, I'll call her later. Now, [look at...]

STAN. [She wants] you to call her as soon as you can.

ALICIA. I'll do it later, you wanna' see what I bought?

STAN. It sounded important.

ALICIA. *(flatly and with purpose)* Do you want to see what I bought?

STAN. *(surrendering)* Yes.

ALICIA. Excellent!

> *(She begins sorting through the shopping bags. Pulling out boxes, other bags, a white teddy bear. As she continues,* **STAN** *picks up the teddy bear and examines it quizzically.)*

I got the most beautiful hair clips. They are perfect, you know, because the dress has the silver stitching? I just have to find them. They're polished metal, but they read perfectly in the light, oh god, they called out to me from across the store, it was serendipitous, it was fate. Okay, I can't find them, but you'll see. And I got something special, but I'm getting ahead of myself. Ah! Here…

> *(She produces a clothing box with a blue bow tied around it. She presents it to him. He's holding the teddy bear. She grabs it away and then re-presents the box to him.)*

I got this, this fantastic package, this box of wonder, for you Stan.

STAN. Oh no.

ALICIA. Oh yes!

STAN. Is it new golf clubs?

ALICIA. Fuck you.

STAN. Nice mouth.

ALICIA. Open it.

STAN. I like it when you talk dirty.

ALICIA. Fucking open it.

> *(He opens the box and pulls out a dark blue polo shirt. He holds it up and looks at it. After a moment…)*

It's a shirt!

STAN. A polo shirt.

ALICIA. A polo shirt!

STAN. Okay.

ALICIA. Because when you meet Daddy at the club, you need to wear a collared shirt, but it's going to be hot outside so long sleeves won't [be the...]

STAN. [I have] shirts.

ALICIA. This is a nice shirt. You'll look better. And all of the men there wear this kind of thing.

STAN. I told you I'm not going. The public course is fine.

ALICIA. I hate golf and even I know the public course is a wasteland.

STAN. Baby, you know I know how important it is to you that I fit in with your Dad. But that place is just not me. And it feels so odd and clunky to try and be some other guy, ya' know? At a restaurant, at your folks' house, when they come here, I can do that; I'm all over it. That should really be enough for him. I mean, I'm not a hanging out with guys kinda' guy. He never even invites me to that club; you invite me because you want me to fit there. He gets it. He's fine. I'm not that guy.

(**ALICIA** *inhales deeply, preps and then launches in...*)

ALICIA. Okay. I don't want you to feel like something you're not. And I know what you think, but it would make him happy, even if you don't think so, and making him happy would make me happy. And then I'll make you happy.

STAN. Happy how?

ALICIA. Fucking happy.

STAN. Oh really?

ALICIA. Mm hmm, let me see you in the new shirt. Just get this one [off and...]

(*She begins to unbutton his shirt. He suddenly jerks away.*)

STAN. [No, it's] okay, I like it, I'll wear it. I'll go.

ALICIA. What's wrong?

STAN. Nothing, I should go, you're right.

ALICIA. But I want to see you try it on.

STAN. I will, here give it to me and I'll go put it on. I'll be [right back.]

ALICIA. [Just put] it on here, what's the big deal?

STAN. Nothing. Just, here, give it to me. What?

ALICIA. Okay, you're acting kind of bizarre.

STAN. No.

ALICIA. Yes.

STAN. No.

ALICIA. Yes you are.

STAN. Let's not make this [into a…]

ALICIA. [Wait, oh] god, is this one of those cold feet things that totally snowballs? Is this one of those things that comes out of nowhere: you won't put on the shirt I bought you, and it unlocks some kind of, I don't know, deep thing, and then you just, just leave me at the altar?

STAN. Because of a polo shirt?

ALICIA. That's how it happens.

STAN. That's how it happens where?

ALICIA. I know something's wrong, I can tell.

STAN. I don't have cold feet; I love you more than anything. I just, sometimes I worry about what you would, listen, if you give me the shirt, I'll go and put it on. It's not a big deal; it's that simple.

(He takes the shirt from her.)

ALICIA. Something's wrong. I'm saying it again. To you.

STAN. If I tell you, you wouldn't…Listen, there's, there are things, okay, we don't have to know every single thing about each other in order to be together, right?

ALICIA. I don't like that at all.

STAN. No, now, you're just reacting, take a minute to actually think about it. Do I know every single thing about you, about what's going on in your head?

ALICIA. I guess not.

STAN. And we're still okay.

ALICIA. I'll be okay regardless. I know how to know what to feel about what other people are thinking; you know that.

STAN. What?

ALICIA. Whatever you have to [tell me…]

STAN. [I don't have] anything [to…]

ALICIA. [I want to] know, you're talking about something. I promise, whatever it is, I won't freak out. As long as the wedding's still on, I won't freak out. If the wedding's off, I'll set you on fire and bury you in the yard, but otherwise…

(pause)

STAN. Do you love me?

ALICIA. You know I do.

STAN. I can't believe I'm gonna' just, ugh, give me a minute.

(He exits with the polo shirt. She shakes off the moment.)

ALICIA. I don't understand what this has to do with the shirt, I don't understand any of this and whether you acknowledge it or not you're acting strange. I've seen you with your shirt off, I've seen all of you, I mean, it's not like you have to be shy or anything. Especially around me, it's not like it would be the first time….

*(**ALICIA** is interrupted, her words stuck in her throat, as **STAN** enters in women's lingerie, some kind of bustier top and panties.)*

STAN. So, um…

(pause)

ALICIA. Are you joking? You're joking.

STAN. Sometimes I dress like this. Under my clothes.

ALICIA. You're joking.

STAN. I like it. It makes me feel, look, I know it's not easy but this is the thing.

ALICIA. You're joking!!!

STAN. You said you wouldn't freak out. I know it's a lot, but you promised.

(**ALICIA** *begins to hyperventilate and tear up.*)

ALICIA. How was I supposed to know that you, I thought you were trying on the, where's the polo shirt?

STAN. In the, who cares about the polo shirt. Oh no, don't cry. It's [not so bad.]

ALICIA. [Oh my god, what] will people say? What if someone finds out? Fuck. How can [I even…]

STAN. [No one's] gonna' find out.

ALICIA. I found out.

STAN. I told you, you're the only person I've ever told.

ALICIA. That's…nice. I can't believe I'm just finding this out. I can't believe I own that same outfit.

STAN. Look, I know, it's "odd." Or whatever. I just…thought it looked good so I got my own, or had it made. I can't fit into your size obviously, but you should think of [it as a…]

ALICIA. [I have to get] out of here.

STAN. It doesn't have to be a big, no I know how that sounds, but it's not necessarily a big deal.

ALICIA. (*Laughing through her tears, a confused thing, she collects her purse and sunglasses.*) Of course not. Of course not!

STAN. Please don't…

(*She exits.*)

Go.

End Scene

5

(VALERIE stands alone.)

VALERIE. Part of preparing, and in case you can't tell I'm one for preparation, but part of that is practice. They just love me down at the firing range, the staff, everyone, even the people who just come in because of some curiosity and then walk right back out the door.

(She laughs at those people.)

But they all love me, especially the regulars. And there are regulars, regular shooters. I'm a regular. I think it's because I smile more than most of the people on the way in. Which, in my everyday life, is not the case. But at the range, in that drab concrete building, I feel good. Drab is generous too, huh, believe me drab is a compliment. Point of fact: I've never seen another black woman there. Ever. Really, I don't think I've ever seen another black person there. That's all right though, I'm used to mostly being around white people. I really don't even notice anymore. But it wouldn't matter if it were all blue people, because every step I take is one step farther away from phone messages from my mother, that tiny apartment, my ridiculous roommate, my uninspired life. Do you have any idea what it's like to work in the Accounts Payable department? All of it just falls away. Click.

The first time I fired a gun was at the range. If you can believe it, I went with my boyfriend at the time. He insisted it was the perfect date, which was informative about that ill-fated relationship on a lot of levels really. He's gone; the gun's still here. I didn't start with rifles of course, although they're my favorites now, started out with a little thing, don't even remember the name. But that first shot, the recoil through my arms, everything getting tight and the tremor down my spine. Amazing. Have you ever had one of those moments where everything tilts just ever so slightly and one thing suddenly makes all the other things somehow feel better? For me, it's pulling the trigger. Click. And then the guns get bigger and the kick gets stronger and I start to feel flush from the excitement of the metal and the purpose and the force and the strength and I want more, you always want more, and I'm, before I know it, I'm there every day. You think you know yourself and then, just, smiling. Because it's different than all the rest of it, I'm different, powerful, in charge. And to shoot at something alive, not just a paper target, I can't even imagine. Making decisions, more important decisions, life and death decisions. How must that feel?

End Scene

6

(**ALICIA**, *disheveled, cautiously enters the lingerie shop under the bell.* **JIMMY** *sits on his stool drinking tea out of an oversized mug.*)

(**ALICIA** *reaches up and flips her fingers across the bell as she passes under it. It is not a conscious thing, as if the door had simply caused the bell to ring.*)

(*At the sound of the bell,* **JIMMY** *stirs…*)

JIMMY. Come in. Don't be shy. I know it seems small but we've got more in here than you could possibly imagine.

(**ALICIA** *takes a few more steps, trying to put herself in order.*)

ALICIA. Hello.

JIMMY. Lovely morning.

ALICIA. What?

JIMMY. It's a lovely morning outside.

ALICIA. Is it?

JIMMY. How can I help you?

ALICIA. I don't know.

JIMMY. Well, what are you looking for?

ALICIA. I don't know.

(**JIMMY** *drinks from his mug.*)

JIMMY. Hm. Well it's not the first time I've been in this situation. Perhaps you can tell me what you hope to achieve with the lingerie and I can better assist you?

ALICIA. I don't even know what I'm doing here.

JIMMY. I get that a lot. But it doesn't matter what apprehension you come in with, as soon as you put something on, the right something, you feel completely different. I know it sounds a little pie in the sky, but I see it happen every day. Well, everyday except Monday. We're closed on Monday.

ALICIA. I was wandering around the city all night and I just...

JIMMY. Ended up here?

ALICIA. Yes.

JIMMY. I've seen you before though, haven't I? You've bought from me, I'm sure. I never forget a face. A few times right? And one of them was, uh, leopard print. Oh, don't cry.

ALICIA. No, I'm not. That's right, you're right. I have been in before. And...I think my fiancé shops here too.

JIMMY. Something beautiful for you?

ALICIA. No.

JIMMY. Actually, we don't carry men's apparel.

ALICIA. No. I think my fiancé "shops" here.

JIMMY. Oh.

ALICIA. Custom made, he said. Just like mine. Just like mine. And I know I bought mine...here.

JIMMY. Well...we do our best to satisfy all needs. Did it look all right? Men's bodies are just totally different animals, you know? I always worry even though it always turns out well.

ALICIA. He was wearing women's lingerie.

JIMMY. But other than that, did it look all right?

ALICIA. He shouldn't be wearing it.

JIMMY. Why not?

ALICIA. Because that's not what men do!

JIMMY. Okay. I'm not sure yelling at me is going to help you very much with your current situation.

(**ROSE** *enters in a silk robe.*)

ROSE. You know, you're right, I think this one is perfect.

(*She stops when she sees* **ALICIA**. *Pause.* **ROSE** *self-consciously adjusts the robe, pulling it tight around her.*)

Hi. Hi, I was just, hi. This is so embarrassing, what are you doing here?

ALICIA. It looks nice, Rose.

JIMMY. It does, doesn't it?

ROSE. Oh no, I feel so silly. I was just heading home and I thought, "What the hey?!" I have so much to tell you about my trip, you won't believe it. I called last night, did Stan give you my, are you, is something wrong?

ALICIA. I didn't know you shopped here, too.

ROSE. Well you spoke so highly about the shop and I finally have a reason to actually buy something sexy so…

(**ALICIA** *bursts into tears.* **ROSE** *crosses to embrace her.*)

Oh god. Oh god, what's wrong?

ALICIA. Everyone shops here!

JIMMY. Please don't get the silk wet.

ROSE. Oh god.

(**ROSE** *jerks away from* **ALICIA**.)

ALICIA. Stan wears women's underwear. He wears it all the time.

ROSE. Oh god.

ALICIA. He just decided to show me.

ROSE. Oh god.

JIMMY. It's only lingerie.

ALICIA. Thank you!!

ROSE. Alicia, don't yell.

JIMMY. You're going to disturb the other customers.

ALICIA. What other customers?!

ROSE. Come here for a minute honey, just calm down and try to take a breath.

(*They step away from* **JIMMY**. *He picks up his mug again, but is clearly listening in on the women.*)

Now, breathe. Are you breathing? You're turning red; breathe.

(**ALICIA** *exhales and then inhales deeply.*)

ALICIA. I'm sorry.

ROSE. It's okay. What, exactly, did Stan say?

ALICIA. We were talking about the wedding and about knowing each other and then, just...bam!

ROSE. Okay. Okay. Okay, well...that sucks. But, okay, he still wants to get married, right?

ALICIA. *(examining her engagement ring, in her own little world...)* I don't know.

ROSE. Did he say he didn't?

ALICIA. Look at this ring.

ROSE. Did he say he didn't want to get married?

ALICIA. No.

ROSE. Just that he...has some unusual fashion tastes.

ALICIA. What would people say? If people found out?

ROSE. What people?

(**ALICIA** *snaps back into the moment.*)

ALICIA. Oh fuck! I told you, I shouldn't have told you, you can't tell anyone.

ROSE. Who am I gonna' tell?

ALICIA. You can't tell anyone.

ROSE. I won't.

ALICIA. You either.

JIMMY. We pride ourselves on our discretion.

ROSE. See, so your secret won't leave this shop.

ALICIA. He acted like it was no big deal, but I could tell he was afraid.

ROSE. Well, that's quite a secret, I don't want to minimize it or anything, but...

ALICIA. But what?

ROSE. I mean, he's a good guy, Alicia. I've finally got a good guy, maybe, and so now I know Stan is one of the good ones. And he's not a jerk or abusive or anything.

ALICIA. It's freakish, isn't it?

ROSE. Actually, the more I think about it, the more it doesn't really seem like a big deal.

JIMMY. That's what I was saying.

ROSE. I've got this, Jimmy.

JIMMY. Sorry.

ROSE. It's just like, I don't know, if he wanted to do something weird in bed. Is it, is it that kind of thing?

ALICIA. I don't know, I don't know anything. I just left, he was standing there and, I mean, what was I supposed to say?

ROSE. So, then, it might not be so bad, once you get all the facts. You should go home and talk to him.

ALICIA. I think he'll look different. He was always so... "guy." I wish you could have seen him. No I don't. You can't say anything.

ROSE. I said I wouldn't, I promise.

JIMMY. I know it's not my place...

(The **WOMEN** *look to him. He picks up his mug and walks over to them while talking.)*

You're upset and that's awful. But, in reality, nothing happened to you. I mean, you seem to have this ever-expanding idea of what would happen to you if people found out, these people, this larger idea of "people" and what they would think. But none of that happened. Your fiancé shared a secret with you; that's all. If he spent his life capturing neighborhood cats, torturing and skinning them and dumping their carcasses in your storage room would that be worse?

(Pause. He waits...)

Yes, of course that would be worse, stay with me here. That would make him a fledgling serial killer, that's worse. It's a matter of perspective and I can tell by your shoes, manicure and hair cut that you have a very specific perspective. And by specific I mean narrow. Sorry. So just ask yourself this: how did he actually look in the lingerie? Not by society's standards, which are all a total façade anyway, but in the absence of what you think other "people" would say: How did he look? He came in here in need of something specific. And whatever he found doesn't make him any less of a man unless you treat him like less of a man. And that's something you choose. I think the fact that he was willing to share that part of his life, his person, with you, a part he might not even understand himself, well, that takes a real man. He was brave. I'd call that brave. I mean it was a lot of things, but definitely brave. And remember, above all else: he has good taste.

ALICIA. Good taste.

JIMMY. That's important, right?

ALICIA. I feel dizzy.

ROSE. Keep breathing. Now look, my new man, he's, he is so mysterious and very European, so you know, kind of femme, but in a masculine way, I don't know, I find it fascinating. But, like I said, I really think he's a good one. And so is your man, I believe that.

ALICIA. Rose, how do, how do you have a new man? You just got back from Spain three seconds ago.

ROSE. I found him in Spain. Amazing, right? I don't know if he's, I mean I gonna find out if he's the, just, don't worry about it; I've got that under control. You look a little better. Can I maybe take you out for coffee? Or vodka?

ALICIA. Can we not talk about it?

ROSE. Don't you want to sort [through...]

ALICIA. [Can we] not talk about it please?

ROSE. Well, that will be kinda', wait, I'll show you pictures from my trip.

JIMMY. I saw them; they're great. Lots of culture.

ALICIA. Well, fine, Spain it is.

(She begins to exit and then stops, adjusting the robe.)

ROSE. Nobody's perfect, Alicia. We do the best we can with what we've got. It's just something to think about, ya' know? Okay, that was totally the last thing I'll say about it.

End Scene

7

(VALERIE polishes her gun while singing a song to herself. She is engrossed in the task and the song reflects both her passion for and fascination with the gun.)

(This goes on a bit, a labor of love.)

(She finishes and examines her work.)

VALERIE. You look so good. No, that's not how you look. You look ready. I'm ready too. Let's go see how this feels.

End Scene

8

(MIGUEL sits in ROSE's apartment. The huge collection of luggage is still there.)

(There is a knock at the door. MIGUEL looks in the direction but doesn't move.)

(Another knock. MIGUEL rises, but doesn't go to answer it. He seems unsure what to do. And then NICOLE enters…)

NICOLE. Rose? Rose, I used my key. If you tell me to be here at seven, then you should, oh! Oh, I'm sorry. I was looking for Rose. Obviously, I mean obviously, sorry.

(pause)

Is she here?

(pause)

Is Rose here?

MIGUEL. No està aquì.

NICOLE. Is that a no? No, she's not here?

MIGUEL. No.

NICOLE. Okay, all right, well…I'll come back.

(Pause. She starts to leave. She stops and come back to her spot.)

Or I might just wait?

(pause)

I'm sure she'll be back soon. I'll wait. So, how are you, are you enjoying your trip, getting to see a lot of, you don't understand me at all do you? I'm so sorry.

(pause)

I see she still hasn't unpacked, I'll never know how she does it.

(NICOLE points to the bags. MIGUEL laughs with a shrug.)

NICOLE. *(cont.)* Well at least we kind of understand at each other. That's something I guess. Jesus, this is like pulling teeth.

(NICOLE sits down in one of the chairs. MIGUEL also sits.)

You don't mind if I talk anyway do you? Even though, I mean, it feels so awkward to just sit here.

(pause)

What to talk about? You don't care.

(Pause. NICOLE looks him over and then, meeting his gaze, looks away. She notices the Jameson's bottle is still present. She pours herself a glass and drinks it in one gulp.)

So this is funny. No, never mind.

(pause)

Okay, I had a dream about you. And I mean I've only met you once, so I'd never tell you of course, but...?

(She shrugs. He smiles and mimics her.)

Right. And I can't talk to Rose about it, I can't talk to anyone about it really. Except you, which is pointless. Ugh. So, okay, I had this dream about you. Have this dream, I'm still having it. It's pretty racy, I don't usually have those kinds of dreams. This is ridiculous. I was there, of course I'm there, and you're there. And you're dressed like a matador, which isn't really a stretch. But you look good. You still look good, but in the outfit I mean. With this amazing red cape. And no shirt on, but I think that was my brain editorializing a little.

(She laughs awkwardly. He laughs back, but it looks like a guess.)

But I'm, I'm not sure, but I think I'm the bull? I'm almost definitely the bull, charging around you and my head feels so heavy because of the horns which seem massive, seriously, these horns I never knew I had and never wanted and then I'm charging right at you and then, instead of fighting we're…well, we're not fighting.

(She laughs. He stares at her.)

NICOLE. *(cont.)* I don't know what to tell you. But I've had that dream every night since you and Rose came back. It just kind of takes over, like it's going to happen no matter what, but I want it to happen even though it's going to happen anyway and, and I wake up breathing heavy and…

*(***MIGUEL*** *gets up and crosses to her.)*

Oh, do you need something? Is there…

(He leans in and kisses her deeply in one swift motion.)

Wow. Wow. Wait, I mean no. No is what I meant. Rose wouldn't like it; she thinks you're…

(He kisses her again.)

MIGUEL. Te gusta…?

NICOLE. I don't understand. What about Rose?

MIGUEL. No.

NICOLE. No?

MIGUEL. No.

NICOLE. No.

MIGUEL. No.

NICOLE. Does she know that?

MIGUEL. Estàs soñando.

NICOLE. I don't [understand.]

MIGUEL. [Lo estàs] soñando ahora.

NICOLE. I think I should…go. I [don't…]

*(As ***MIGUEL*** continues through this next bit, he begins to hold ***NICOLE***, kiss her neck, unbutton or remove some of her clothing basically she is overwhelmed.)*

MIGUEL. [Déjame] decirte esto: Cuando besé tu mano, dejé una marca que se hundió en tu piel, hasta llegar a tu sangre. La marca se arrastró hasta tu corazón y pasó de ventrículo en ventrículo, revolviéndose en la corriente.

NICOLE. [Okay.]

MIGUEL. [Y la] marca se expulsó, moviéndose de nuevo, avanzando por todo tu cuerpo, llegando hasta tu pecho, tu cuello, pasando por tu boca y tus labios; justo debajo de la superficie.

NICOLE. Okay, [okay.]

MIGUEL. [La marca] pasó por tus ojos, tu sien y tu nuca, hasta entrar en tu mente. Ahí se ancló, convirtiéndose en un pensamiento, y el pensamiento se volvió un sueño, y el sueño en sentimiento: deseo, sólo deseo. Y ahora está aquí: el sueño, el deseo. Y como no tienes elección, debes ceder. ¿Por qué no ceder? La marca, el sueño. Tú y yo, ahora, en este momento. Estás soñando. Y yo terminaré con tu sueño. Eso voy a hacer.

(He pulls her up. He picks her up into a cradle. She cannot look away from him. She never really had a chance. He carries her off to the bedroom.)

End Scene

9

(blackout)

(A gunshot, a large rifle sounds in the dark.)

(Lights slowly rise to reveal **VALERIE** *sitting in a crouched position, head down; knees held to her chest. She rocks a bit, clearly crying.)*

(The gun sits on the floor a few feet away, just outside the light.)

End Scene

10

*(**STAN** is in his lingerie panties and a bathrobe. He holds jeans and the polo shirt. The teddy bear still sits on the couch near the discarded bustier.)*

STAN. The first time I met Alicia, she looked perfect. I mean every single thing, no wrinkles on any piece of clothing, everything tailored, not a hair out of place. She was smiling, giving someone directions. And I stopped. I literally stopped. And I was running on a treadmill at the time, facing out the front window of the gym. So when I stopped…? Wham! I was thrown right off the end. I broke my headphones and everyone around me was startled in that trying not to laugh kind of way. It was ridiculous. I looked ridiculous. Of course, Alicia doesn't know this story. I think that would have been the end of it, right there, before it even got started. But as far as first impressions go, she definitely made the right one.

And when I think back on it, she was also holding a shopping bag too. So, essentially, there was everything about Alicia, wrapped up in that one image: looking perfect, smiling, helping someone else while shopping. That makes her sound simpler than she is actually. She's amazing. And that first moment is so important, you know?

*(**STAN** removes the robe and picks up a pair of jeans to get dressed. **ALICIA** enters hesitantly, removing her sunglasses. She stops at the sight of **STAN**. He freezes, holding the jeans, exposed again. **ALICIA** shakes her head and rushes off. **STAN** hangs his head.)*

(He slips on a pair of jeans.)

I've admittedly had to work around my fashion choices during our time together. It's funny; I had it down to a science. It's always when you stop thinking about something for the briefest, or start to feel comfortable. I mean, how many times have you suddenly been asked to take your shirt off. Or commanded to take your shirt off. Think about it. And I, okay, ya' know, maybe I wanted to get caught. I don't think I did, but I could have figured a way out of it, talked around it. Or maybe I couldn't keep looking at her and knowing, self- sabotage. I don't think I'm that kind of guy, but I never thought Alicia was the kind of girl I would want, or would want me and so I don't really know who I am lately. Or without her.

(He pulls the polo shirt over his head. He adjusts the shirt.)

STAN. *(cont.)* That moment? That moment sucked. I don't know what I was thinking would happen, but her face was so, I mean the look in her eyes. It's something I do for me and I never meant for it to be so "on display." Because it's not that kind of thing, it's not an attention kind of thing. It's a private thing. But she looked at me like I was some kind of bizarre animal in the zoo. Some exotic thing and I'm not that, I'm the opposite of exotic.

(He sits down on the couch and picks up the white teddy bear, holding it to his chest. He almost looks like a little boy.)

She'll come around. I mean, we're getting married. Alicia wouldn't pass up that party for anything. I hope. Oh god I know how that sounds, listen, it's not so bad, not a big deal. And I can change. Maybe. No, I can. I'm just a regular guy, underneath it all, right? Just look at me.

End Scene

11

*(**ROSE** enters her apartment with a small bag. She crosses through the room.)*

ROSE. Miguel, are you here? I know you can't understand me but boy do I have a surprise for you. Wait until you see me in this...

*(She stops abruptly and enters again, slowly. **NICOLE** rushes in after her wrapped in a red bed sheet.)*

NICOLE. Rose, it's not what you think, I mean it is what you think and I can't explain it but I'm sorry, I just got carried away and he [was so...]

ROSE. [I bought] something pretty to wear.

NICOLE. Are you okay?

*(**ROSE** spins and glares at **NICOLE.**)*

No, obviously not okay, what I [mean is...]

ROSE. [Shut-up!!]

*(**MIGUEL** enters casually and stands behind **NICOLE**, jeans open and shirt in hand.)*

Look at you.

NICOLE. I'm so [sorry.]

ROSE. [I'm not] talking to you!!

*(**ROSE** crosses past **NICOLE** to **MIGUEL.**)*

NICOLE. Okay.

ROSE. I don't understand. Not even a little bit. Can you explain it to me? No, of course you can't. Of course you can't, I'm such a fucking idiot. Am I an idiot Nicole, is that what you think?

NICOLE. No one [thinks that.]

ROSE. [I swear to] God, Nicole, I do not want to hear your voice right now. I'm talking to Miguel. We're talking, right? I'm talking and you're just standing there. Do you get even a little how fucked up this is?

*(**MIGUEL** looks to **NICOLE**, confused.)*

ROSE. *(cont.)* Don't look at her, look at me! I'm the one who paid for everything in Spain, who brought you here, who bought god damned lingerie to try and look good for you and you know I did that because I thought you were, we were, I don't care if you can't understand me you knew what was going on. And so did Nicole.

(As she is talking, he puts a hand to her cheek. She smacks it away.)

I am an idiot. I'm an idiot.

NICOLE. Rose, you're not.

ROSE. I should have gone to Africa with Valerie.

NICOLE. Let me get dressed and we'll talk about it, all right?

ROSE. Are you serious?

NICOLE. I know it's a bad thing, I don't even understand it myself.

ROSE. Well that's fantastic. Was he good?

NICOLE. Rose.

ROSE. Look at him, I wanna' know.

NICOLE. I don't remember.

ROSE. Oh for fuck's sake.

NICOLE. The whole thing was, just, unreal. Like a dream and I wish [I could…]

ROSE. [I can't] believe you'd do this and then try to act all innocent about it!

NICOLE. No, no, [I'm not.]

ROSE. [I never] even saw it coming. Not from you, Nicole, not this. I mean, he's European, so I should have guessed [that…]

NICOLE. [Rose stop] it, you can't keep making these sweeping judgments about people all the time just because [they might…]

ROSE. [Oh your timing] is just perfect! Please do deconstruct for me how closed-minded I am while sweating from the exertion of fucking the man I love, loved, thought I loved, whatever.

NICOLE. You have to believe me, I never [meant to…]

ROSE. [I want] you to get dressed and get out. And if you're so good at communicating with him, tell him to get out too. I don't care; just get out. I have to go return something. Something silly. When I get back, you should both be gone.

NICOLE. You can't just leave, we've been best friends for years.

ROSE. Say that again.

NICOLE. What? We've been best friends [for…]

ROSE. [Exactly.]

(*ROSE exits. **NICOLE** collapses into one of the chairs and begins to cry.*)

NICOLE. What was I thinking?

MIGUEL. Don't be sad.

NICOLE. Ugh, what did I do?

MIGUEL. You had a fantasy.

NICOLE. I don't, what?

(*She looks up at **MIGUEL**.*)

MIGUEL. It seems like I should get my things and go.

(*He puts on his shirt.*)

NICOLE. You speak English?!?! You, where are you going? You can't just leave.

MIGUEL. When the matador finishes the bullfight, he doesn't stay and chat with the bull. He kills it. And then he goes home.

NICOLE. That's terrible.

(***MIGUEL** smiles at her warmly and, with a genuine sense of camaraderie, offers…*)

MIGUEL. It is all a game Nicole; enjoy the sport.

(*He exits.*)

End Scene

12

(VALERIE *stands alone.*)

VALERIE. Have you ever seen a gazelle? Not a live gazelle, I doubt you've seen a live gazelle, but in a video or a photo? They're beautiful. I always imagined myself under a big blue sky, sun beating down, tall yellow and brown grass shifting in the wind. Taking aim at some kind of ferocious thing. I don't know why I imagined that, what kind of ferocious thing? I have no idea. And then the man, the guide, pointed out this herd of gazelle. And I'm not even sure that's legal, to shoot a gazelle. I'm not sure this guide is on the up and up. But I'm there, under the big blue sky, sun beating down, tall yellow and brown grass shifting in the wind. And I'm taking aim at this graceful, no, with these brown eyes. It was everything I imagined, except that one thing. I feel like I could see its heart beating in its chest through the scope of the gun. I picked, of course I bought the best scope. And after coming so far, spending all of this money, just for a second, the wind stopped and I didn't know what I would do. I didn't even see the gazelle, I saw...

I pulled the trigger. Click. And it wasn't like the firing range; I didn't even feel the punch of the gun into my shoulder. Even the sound of the gun came from somewhere far away. Except for the trigger. Click. So loud and the air around me, the air started unfolding, from the sound, out of the sound. Click. And then this continuous unfolding, image after image through the air, the sky disappearing, a new picture unfolding, everything unfolding, flip, flip, flip, and then click: I'm standing at the counter of this strange store, lingerie everywhere.

(JIMMY *appears on his stool.*)

I'm serious, I have no idea; it's crazy, I'm crazy.

JIMMY. Oh, uh…

(He hops off his stool, crosses over, flips the bell with his hand causing it to ring and hops back on his stool in one fluid motion.)

Sorry about that, you slipped right past me. How can I help you today?

VALERIE. What?

JIMMY. I bet I can guess your size without measuring. We custom fit everything. Do you know what you're looking for?

VALERIE. I don't need anything. I'm not even, what is this?

JIMMY. Everyone needs something.

VALERIE. Leave me alone.

JIMMY. Something to help you see yourself in a whole new light?

VALERIE. I see myself just fine. I'm fine.

JIMMY. How about those parts you don't really like?

VALERIE. Excuse me?

JIMMY. Problem areas? You can't make them go away, but you can learn to love them. You should love them. You'll look great. Oh! What about satin?

VALERIE. I love everything about myself. Get out of my grassland, this is my, you're ruining my vacation.

JIMMY. Is it a grassland?

VALERIE. Yes.

JIMMY. I think it's a savannah.

VALERIE. What is going on?!

JIMMY. Let's stop and think: Where are you? What are you shooting at?

VALERIE. I'm here, not here, I'm in Kenya, I'm shooting my gun, I picked out this gun, I'm shooting [at…]

JIMMY. [You're] shooting [at?]

VALERIE. [I'm] shooting [at…]

JIMMY. [You're] shooting [at?]

VALERIE. [Stop it!] I'm shooting at...

(pause)

JIMMY. It's all right. I'll be here when you get back. You'll still be here too.

VALERIE. And then, gone, all of it, pieces falling out of the air with sunshine and grasslands behind them. And I'm looking down at this bloody gazelle. And it's not even dead yet, I didn't hit it in the right place. So they had to... I'm going home.

(then quickly...)

Oh lord, I don't want to go home. I don't want to carry this back. I didn't come here looking for myself, I said that, I meant it. So I am done with this vacation. Like I said, like Disneyland, you go home. And you forget the rides made you sick, you only remember the good parts. But I will never, in my life, forget how that felt. Click.

End Scene

13

(STAN sits on the couch nervously. Maybe he holds the teddy bear, maybe it's just around somewhere. He gets up, paces a bit, sits again. ALICIA enters. STAN is immediately on his feet.)

(pause)

ALICIA. Sorry I ran out and all, I [just…]

STAN. [It's okay.]

(Pause. They are still.)

ALICIA. I was out walking around.

STAN. Long walk. Two days.

(pause)

ALICIA. Can you sit down, you look like you don't know whether to tackle me or I don't even know, just sit down, okay?

STAN. I can do that.

(STAN sits.)

Are you going to sit?

ALICIA. I don't know.

STAN. Okay.

ALICIA. Yes.

(She sits at the other end of the couch. She's having a hard time looking at STAN, so mostly she doesn't.)

I'm sitting. We're sitting.

(Pause. STAN fidgets some. He takes a deep breath and…)

STAN. I should have told you instead of showing you but I thought it would be kind of like a "pulling off the Band-Aid" kind of thing and you were so adamant about wanting to know even though there's no way you could know what you wanted to know, not that I'm blaming you for wanting you know, I thought you had a right to know, you needed to know, before anything went any further and so that's why I showed you, but I should have just told you. I'm sorry.

(**ALICIA** *begins to laugh, it is small and sad; it isn't funny.*)

STAN. *(cont.)* It's not funny.

ALICIA. No, it's not.

STAN. Then why are you laughing?

(She stops.)

ALICIA. I'm glad you told me, showed me. I'm not glad. But…this is so bizarre. I don't even know how to talk to you about, I don't [even know.]

STAN. [Just ask me] anything that [you think is…]

ALICIA. [Is it a sex] thing?

STAN. No.

ALICIA. Are you sure?

STAN. Of course I'm, it's not a sex thing. It doesn't have anything to do with sex.

ALICIA. Okay.

STAN. I mean, it feels good. But not like that.

ALICIA. Do you do it all the time?

STAN. No.

ALICIA. When?

STAN. When I can get away with it. I know how that sounds, but that's when I do it.

ALICIA. Could you stop?

STAN. Do I have to?

ALICIA. Would you?

STAN. If it meant making you happy, I would try.

ALICIA. Try?

STAN. I would stop.

ALICIA. Except when you can get away with it. Okay, I knew you couldn't be perfect. I kept saying to myself, there's no way a guy can be this perfect. And I'm not perfect, I'm not saying that I'm, ugh…

(pause)

Why do you do it?

STAN. Because it feels good, I said that.

ALICIA. No, how does it feel good, in what way? Be specific because I'm having a hard time with this question and answer thing, just tell me, okay?

STAN. I like the way it feels. Wait, I know, I'm getting more specific. It feels like something I should wear. It's the same as putting on my watch or my favorite hat; it feels comfortable. And safe. Safe? I don't know where that came from, but I guess that's close. And I feel…ugh, okay, fine, I'll just, I feel attractive when I have it on. Even though no one can see it, I feel attractive and so I kind of have a…

ALICIA. Swagger.

STAN. Sure.

ALICIA. If you had given me all the guesses in the world, I never would have figured out that's where you get your swagger. But that's, so, it's a little bit of a sex thing.

STAN. Well not a sex act thing, but it's sexy. In my, I mean, I think it's sexy. But I know you don't share that [particular opinion.]

ALICIA. [Well I only saw you] for a minute. Not even, just a second really. So I don't know how it looks, because I just sort of looked away or didn't, my eyes went out of focus, so I don't know how it looks.

STAN. Well would you, would you want to see it again?

ALICIA. I don't…are you, you're not wearing anything now are you?

STAN. No.

ALICIA. Oh.

STAN. Maybe.

ALICIA. Maybe?

(He gets up and undoes his pants exposing the under-wear.)

STAN. Just, okay, just the underwear but only because I was upset [and didn't…]

ALICIA. [It's okay, it's] okay stop.

(He sits again.)

STAN. Don't call off the wedding.

ALICIA. I don't know why I care so much about what other people might think.

STAN. Don't call off the wedding.

ALICIA. It would be such a great party.

STAN. And I do love you. And you love me, even with my quirks.

ALICIA. Quirk. You look good in that shirt.

STAN. Thanks.

ALICIA. That I picked out.

STAN. Yes.

ALICIA. That I made you wear. I'm sorry, I know in my mind that it shouldn't be a big deal but it still feels like a big deal. But you still feel right, too.

STAN. That's good.

ALICIA. No, it's just confusing. This all feels, I don't know, so…so you have to be patient.

STAN. Patient?

ALICIA. We still have a, clearly we still have a lot to learn about each other.

STAN. I'll do anything.

ALICIA. Yes.

STAN. Anything.

ALICIA. Yes.

STAN. What do you want me to do?

(pause)

ALICIA. No leopard print.

STAN. Stop it.

ALICIA. I am the only one that gets to wear leopard [print.]

STAN. [Alicia,] don't joke [about it.]

ALICIA. [I think] I'm being serious, but it's such a hard thing to be serious about. Lingerie.

(Pause. After a moment he gently turns her face to his.)

STAN. All right then: no leopard print.

(He begins to kiss her, but holds off. She brings her mouth to his.)

(They lean back onto the couch in an embrace and are frozen in tableau on stage.)

End Scene

14

(**NICOLE** *enters. She is still wrapped in the red sheet from earlier, only now it is incredibly long. As* **NICOLE** *begins,* **JIMMY** *dresses the edges of the sheet so that it fills the space around* **NICOLE**.)

(*She is aware of* **JIMMY**, *offering him bits of the story until he finishes with the sheet.*)

NICOLE. I don't usually have these kinds of dreams. I'm there. And he's there, dressed like a matador. He looks good. Good's not the word. He looks imminent, unavoidable, like a collision with no breaks. But no cape, I'm wrapped in his red cape. I'm still the bull, definitely the bull, charging around and my head feels so heavy because of the horns which are more massive by the moment, these horns I never knew I had and still never wanted and then I'm charging right at him, but out of the corner of my eye I see something.

(**JIMMY** *is finished, the red sheet swallowing the floor. He vanishes.*)

In the crowd of people, in the stands of the arena, something catches my eye. It's too far away to see, but I see it anyway. Rose. She's sitting with her large sun hat on. Miguel next to her, not the Miguel from my dream, but Rose's Miguel. He takes her hand.

(**ROSE** *enters still carrying the robe. She hesitates, begins to exit but then turns and walks to* **NICOLE**. **NICOLE** *begins to speak and* **ROSE** *slaps her, hard, across the face.* **ROSE** *exits.*)

(**NICOLE** *pulls the sheet tight.*)

But Rose won't look at me. She can't look at me. So I can't look at her and be all the things I am. Because I don't know why I did that and I don't think I would do that, it's not me. It's not. So with all of the effort I can muster I turn my head with the gigantic horns back towards the matador only to feel his blade slice deep into my chest. It misses the heart. But only just. A nick, a small cut, so that everything will spill out over time as I lay there wrapped in my red sheet, in my bull body.

NICOLE. *(cont.)* I don't remember agreeing to play this game. Even though I agreed. It just kind of took over, like it was going to happen no matter what, but I wanted it to happen even though I shouldn't, even though it was going to happen anyway. And it does. It is. I am. And then it's done. And I miss her.

*(**NICOLE** collects some of the sheet over her arm and trails to the edge of the stage. Before exiting, with her back to the audience and the sheet spilling around her, she is frozen onstage.)*

End Scene

15

(ROSE sits alone in her apartment holding the silk robe she purchased earlier. Maybe she's drinking Jameson's again. Maybe she's been drinking. MIGUEL's suitcases are gone, but hers remain. They are still packed.)

(VALERIE enters with her single, well-packed bag. She doesn't notice ROSE.)

ROSE. Welcome home.

VALERIE. Oh! Oh, I thought you'd be at work. I mean, thank you.

ROSE. How was your trip?

VALERIE. Fine. Why aren't you at work?

ROSE. I'm…sick.

VALERIE. I hope it's nothing catching.

ROSE. You'll be fine. Anyway, didn't you, like, get inoculated against everything for your trip? You wouldn't shut-up about all those shots.

VALERIE. I didn't get inoculated against your attitude.

(She smiles, a plastic thing, and sets down her bag. ROSE doesn't acknowledge the smile and simply charges ahead.)

ROSE. Listen, you've only been back for two minutes, I [don't need…]

VALERIE. [Exactly.] Exactly, I come in the door exhausted, annoyed from 18 hours on a plane with crying babies, loud crying babies, and you wanna' start something right when I walk in the door? Not even you do that. What is wrong?

ROSE. I'm sorry.

VALERIE. Thank you, that's not what I asked, what kind of sick are you?

ROSE. I'm trying to be nice.

VALERIE. Rose.

ROSE. Love sick.

(**VALERIE** *picks up her bag.*)

VALERIE. I do not have the energy for this right now.

ROSE. I'm serious.

VALERIE. People have real problems Rose, real unhappiness, most people don't need to manufacture reasons to be miserable. I don't understand it.

ROSE. *(She starts crying.)* You're right. I'm such an idiot.

VALERIE. [Um…]

ROSE. [I really] thought it was some kind of magic thing, which sounds so ridiculous, even saying it out loud, I mean he couldn't even speak English, how does that even work?

VALERIE. Look, we don't really have this kind of relationship.

ROSE. What?

VALERIE. A crying relationship.

ROSE. Oh God.

(She pulls it together, embarrassed.)

I didn't mean to do that. You're right.

VALERIE. I'm just…I am dead on my feet and my trip was not…what I expected.

ROSE. Where's your gun? That gigantic gun, you bought that big case and everything.

VALERIE. I lost it.

ROSE. No way.

VALERIE. I left it at the hotel in Nairobi.

ROSE. In Nigeria?

VALERIE. Kenya.

ROSE. Whatever.

VALERIE. It's an entirely different country.

ROSE. I can't believe you left that gun. You were, like, in love with that gun. Can they ship it to you?

VALERIE. It was just a gun. Who was this guy?

ROSE. It doesn't matter. I don't even know where he is anymore. The bus station? Spain? Somewhere with Nicole? I don't care. I don't care.

VALERIE. With Nicole?

ROSE. Listen, no more Nicole. She is off the list. No more Nicole, no more stupid guy. All I've got is this fucking silk robe. Laughable. And I only have it because there's a "no return" policy.

(**JIMMY** *enters, ringing the bell on route to his stool.*)

JIMMY. Oh no, I can't take it back. No returns, that's the policy. Besides, you still need it. Look at you.

ROSE. I don't want it.

JIMMY. It made you feel beautiful, it still will. Trust me, one day it'll be the perfect thing.

ROSE. Fuck you.

JIMMY. Have a nice day.

ROSE. Fuck you.

JIMMY. Have a nice [day.]

ROSE. [I said] fuck you!

JIMMY. Have a nice day.

(He exits.)

ROSE. Fucking customer service.

VALERIE. It's nice.

ROSE. It's stupid.

VALERIE. Listen, I really want to just take a bath and not think about anything. Are you gonna' be okay for now?

ROSE. Valerie, I don't think I ever really gave you a chance in this whole roommate [thing.]

VALERIE. [I have my] share of issues too.

ROSE. No, but I really want you to [know that…]

VALERIE. [I know you're] upset right now. I'm sorry about it. I've kind of got my own thing going on.

ROSE. About the gun?

VALERIE. *(rising to leave...)* Okay, we don't have to be friends just because we live together Rose, all right?

ROSE. Other than losing the gun, did you have a good time?

VALERIE. I told you I'm tired.

ROSE. Please, just tell me a little. Did you see any wild animals or anything?

(pause)

VALERIE. Have you ever, I don't even know why I'm trying to, Rose, I saw a Gazelle. And something inside me felt more alone than I've ever felt in my entire life and then empty and then that empty was filled up by something else, regret, something, I didn't like it, and now I want to get it out, but I'm not sure how. I want to be happy and I know that I'm not now. So yes, fine, I saw a really beautiful Gazelle.

ROSE. Oh. All right. Well, I saw a bullfight. A live one. It was...

*(*VALERIE *exits.)*

It was just okay.

*(Seated at the table, *ROSE *clutches the silk robe to her chest and is frozen onstage, joining the emerging tableau of *ALICIA, STAN *and *NICOLE.*)*

End Scene

16

(**MIGUEL** *stands alone. His suitcases are at his feet, maybe a bag over his shoulder. The sounds of an airplane taking off and airport terminal noise fill the space.*)

MIGUEL. I'll make this brief. Plane to catch and all. Y es un vuelo transatlántico.

Not speaking. Listening. I support that entirely. It's kind of astonishing how much of themselves people will hand over to you to feel comfortable. You don't even have to ask.

You don't have to say a word.

No hablando. Escuchando. La gente pensará más de ti de lo que puedes imaginar. Me convertí en torero al tomar de la mano a una mujer. People will make you more than you could ever imagine, if you let them…

And why not let them?

(*A bright smile, genuinely entertained.*)

Y por qué no dejarles. Todo es un juego. Not speaking. Listening. Playing along. Hablando, no. Escuchando. Convirtiéndote en algo. I find it all so fascinating. My name's not even Miguel. But you know, she never even asked. Not once. Isn't that something? This is what I'm saying to you, give yourself over and you can become anyone.

(*He picks up his bags.*)

Que tengas muy buen viaje.

(**MIGUEL** *begins to exit and just as he reaches the edge of the stage, he is frozen into the tableau.*)

End Scene

17

(JIMMY enters with his big mug of tea in hand. Just like the beginning of the play, he stands near the lingerie rack.)

(He moves freely and with ease amongst the frozen images of the other characters that remain onstage. He casually references them as he speaks.)

JIMMY. I'm sure I've got something that will fit you just right. Make you feel beautiful. What do you think? You should look now, because it's going fast. I mean, it's practically gone.

We specialize in the custom fit, just like a second skin, something to make you feel special. All hand-sewn. Measurements, measurements, every single piece stitched precisely to your need. Of course, that only works when you know what you need. And sometimes, sometimes someone will come in, very nervous, you know, and work up the courage to try something on. It doesn't matter what I recommend, people never take the first thing you recommend. They have to mess up once or twice before they ask for help.

But then, once they've got the perfect piece on, they see themselves in an entirely different way; different person in the mirror looking back. It happens so fast, in a blink, in a glance. Sometimes people like it, mostly they don't. Because that's when you see it, even if it's just for a moment, you know what kind of person you really are. So I mean really, even when it's bad, it's good.

(VALERIE enters cautiously.)

That's how you find out what you're looking for in that dressing room, what you need. And once that's done…

(She reaches up, still examining the store and brushes the bell with her hand. The sound attracts JIMMY's attention. He turns but is otherwise still. VALERIE casts her gaze around the store, taking in all of the frozen characters as if they were manikins.)

VALERIE. *(quietly)* I don't believe this.

JIMMY. Hello.

VALERIE. Oh! I'm sorry, this, this is like a bit of a déjà vu.

JIMMY. Déjà vu?

VALERIE. Déjà vu.

JIMMY. *(with a laugh...)* Déjà vu.

VALERIE. I didn't think this place would really be here?

JIMMY. Been here for a while. Take your time. Watch your step.

VALERIE. I'm looking for something, it's just, well, I'm not exactly sure what I need.

JIMMY. Don't you worry; I get that all the time.

(blackout.)

End of Play

Also by
Steve Yockey...

Bright. Apple. Crush.

Cartoon

Octopus

Subculture

Please visit our website **samuelfrench.com** for complete descriptions and licensing information.

OTHER TITLES AVAILABLE FROM SAMUEL FRENCH

SUBCULTURE

Steve Yockey

Ten Minute Plays / Various m and f

Two men at the end of the world, a woman who believes she turns children to stone, some college students with alcohol and a sledge-hammer, the perpetrator of a hit-and-run accident, a man obsessed with asphyxiation, and a roadside elephant in India. The very broken characters that inhabit this collection of shorts wander through a dimly lit, over stimulated and paranoia-fueled world that exists just underneath the dominant popular culture. From the darkly comic to the starkly distressing, these uneasy little plays are tightly wound, structurally adventurous glimpses into some of the most simultaneously intimate and harrowing moments of everyday life.

Contains:

(every little thing)
sucker punch
kiss & tell
dizziness & loss of breath
snuff film
lonesome
stop motion
swallow
(stereo) headphones
medusa

OTHER TITLES AVAILABLE FROM SAMUEL FRENCH

OCTOPUS

Steve Yockey

5m / Dark Comedy / Unit Set

After young couple Kevin and Blake engage in an adventurous and hastily planned night of group sex with the older, more "experienced" Max and Andy, they are left trying to salvage their relationship from a pummeling mix of jealousy, betrayal, telegrams from a soaking wet delivery boy and a ravenous sea monster from the ocean floor. This universal love story rendered through a post-modern gay lens slips from domestic comedy into a darkly fantastic fable examining the role and depth of commitment in relationships and what it really means to say the words "I love you."

"A fiercely imaginative and finely tuned new voice... Smartly observed and blissfully performed... [*Octopus*'] tentacles tickle the funny bone, awake the mind and tug on the heart."
– *San Francisco Chronicle*

"An evening full of arresting images… classic tragedy seen through a very contemporary ironic lens"
– *Marin Independent Journal*

"This tale of two gay couples' group sex fling and its serious consequences arrives at a powerful statement about illness and love."
– *Variety*